This Little Tiger book belongs to:

_____

_____

_____

For Elliott, Scarlet, Gabby, Annie and Tilly ~ S S

For my little chick, Ava ~ A G

BIG CATS

LION ~ KING OF THE BEASTS

CRAZY

CROCODILES

come and see the
FABULOUS
FLAMINGOES

McGREW'S
IGUANA

LITTLE TIGER PRESS
1 The Coda Centre, 189 Munster Road, London SW6 6AW
www.littletiger.co.uk

First published in Great Britain 2015
This edition published 2015

Text copyright © Steve Smallman 2015 * Illustrations copyright © Ada Grey 2015
Steve Smallman and Ada Grey have asserted their rights to be identified as the author and illustrator
of this work under the Copyright, Designs and Patents Act, 1988
A CIP catalogue record for this book is available from the British Library

ISBN 978-1-84869-138-4
Printed in China
LTP/1800/1358/0915

10 9 8 7 6 5 4 3

McGREW'S
ZOO

POO IN THE ZOO

Steve Smallman
Ada Grey

LITTLE TIGER PRESS
London

TICKETS

Little Bob McGrew was a keeper at the zoo.

Looking after animals was what he **loved** to do,

But it wasn't always fun, because Bob was the one,

Who had to push a cart around and shovel up the . . .

McGREW'S
ZOO

HEAD KEEPER

...POO!

There was tiger **poo**,
lion **poo**,
prickly porcupine **poo**,

Plummeting giraffe **poop** that landed with a splat,

Dollops of gnu **poo**, bouncy kangaroo **poo**,

A trail of drippy **droppings** from a fat wombat!

WHOOPS!

Flying bits of bat **poo**,
"Crikey, whose is that?" **poo**,

A **pongy** pat of panda **poo**
steaming on the sand.

And Monkey always threw his
as fast as he could do his,

So no one had a clue where
his **poo** might land!

IGUANA iguana

Bob felt dizzy, he was far too busy,
With big jobs and little jobs all around the place.
Then he slipped on a banana,
while mucking out Iguana,
And it ran off with a very greedy grin upon its face!

The lizard caused hysteria inside the cafeteria,
Climbing on the counters, eating **everything** he saw:

Eleven lime lollies,
all the cakes from off the trolleys,

A pepperoni pizza
and then sandwiches galore!

Iguana's bulgy belly
started wobbling like a **jelly,**

"Ooh!" he groaned, "I don't think
I could eat another bite!"

HELP!

Then his **greedy** little eyes
saw some sparkly fireflies,

So he **gobbled them up too**
because he fancied 'something light.'

Iguana said, "Uh-oh!"
as his bum began to glow,

He pulled a funny face
and plopped a **poop** upon the floor!

But Iguana's jaw soon dropped
when he saw the **poop** he'd plopped!

And he ran back to his cage
where Bob was waiting by the door.

Bob turned around and saw
something **glowing** on the floor,

A **poo** that shone so brightly
it was **lighting up his face!**

McGREW'S ZOO

HEAD KEEPER

"No creature in this zoo
has ever done a glowing poo!"

He whispered to himself,
"It must have come from outer space!"

Soon everybody knew about the new **poo** in the zoo,

And people flocked to see the inter-planetary **poop**.

Then a man in a cravat and a sparkly blue top hat

Said, "Hallo there, Mr Zookeeper, my name is Hector Gloop."

"I'm like **you**," said Hector, "I'm another **poo** collector!

I collect exotic **poo-poos**, I've got quite a **big** selection.

I want the world to see how AMAZING **poo** can be!

BE AMAZED!

Please climb aboard my

POO MUSEUM,

I'll show you my collection!"

WELCOME to GLOOP'S POO MUSEUM
GLOOP'S AMAZING POO MUSEUM
IT'S POO TASTIC!
Once in a lifetime!
AMAZING!
SUPER!
WoW!
THIS WAY

CAMEL POO

Worm POO

WARNING!
FIRE ANT
POO
may be hot!

"I've got a pile of yeti **poo**,

and some that's like spaghetti **poo**,

A smoking pile of dragon **poo**,

(they're **very** hard to find!),

A mammoth **poo** in ice,

oh, and this one's **very nice**,

It's a massive pile of **poo-poo**

from a dinosaur's behind!

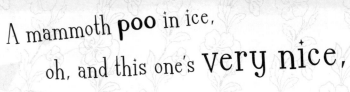
FLY POO

Flamingo Poop

Dragon Poo

SLUG
POO

GRIFFIN
POOP

TOXIC

Tiger Poo

Mouse Poo

DODO
doo-doo

SQUIRREL POO
WARNING MAY CONTAIN NUTS

WOO

I've got huge **poos**, tiny **poos**,
crusty **poos** and shiny **poos**,
Every kind of **poo-poo**,
you could ever wish to see!

Well, I've got some dodo **doo-doo**
but not **glowing poo** like you do,

Oh, I've simply got to have it!
Will you sell your **poo** to me?"

WALRUS *poop*

YETI *poo*

Loch Ness Monster

MAMMOTH

POO

Unicorn Poo

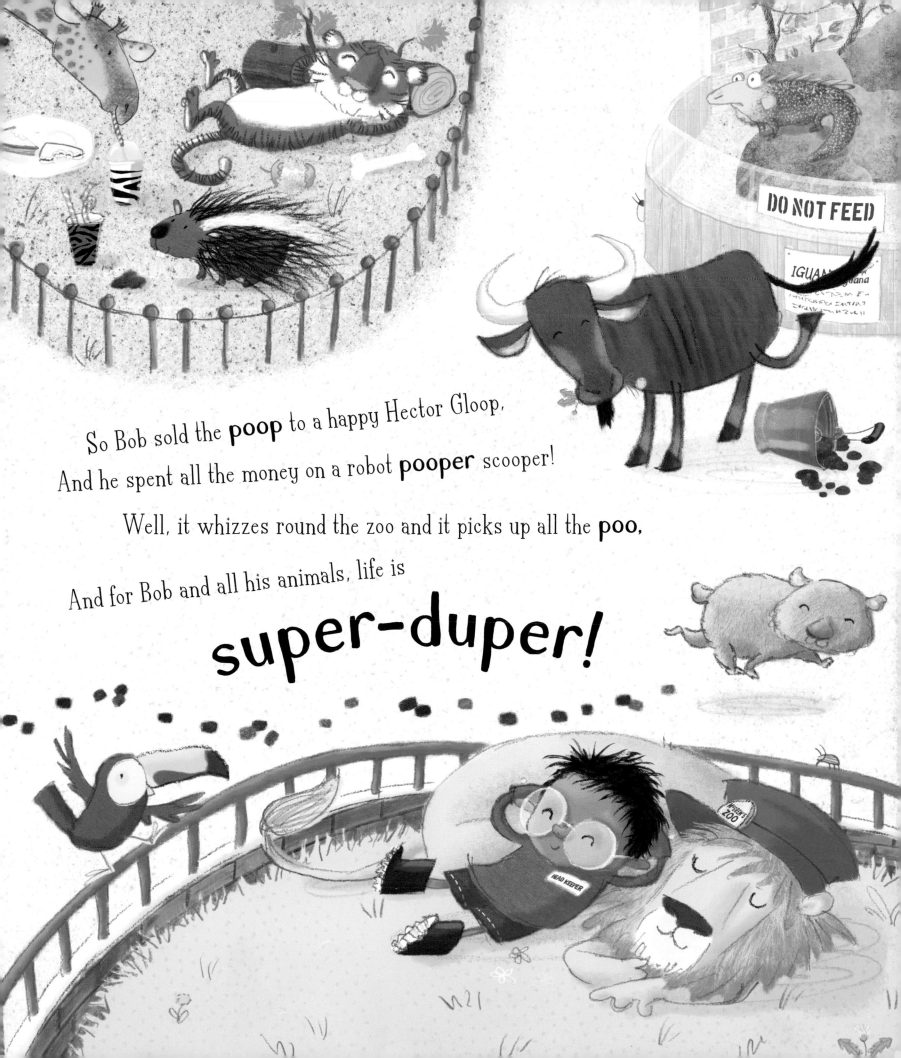

DO NOT FEED

IGUANA

So Bob sold the **poop** to a happy Hector Gloop,
And he spent all the money on a robot **pooper** scooper!

Well, it whizzes round the zoo and it picks up all the **poo**,

And for Bob and all his animals, life is

super-duper!

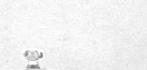

More gloriously gross tales from Little Tiger Press!

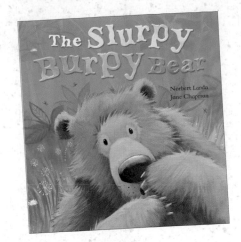

The Slurpy Burpy Bear
Norbert Landa
Jane Chapman

Dragon Stew

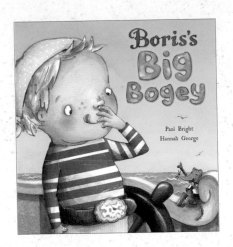

Boris's Big Bogey
Paul Bright
Hannah George

POOH!
IS THAT YOU, BERTIE?
David Roberts

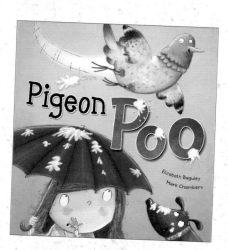

Pigeon Poo
Elizabeth Baguley
Mark Chambers

Mighty Mo
ALISON BROWN

For information regarding any of the above titles or for our catalogue, please contact us:
Little Tiger Press, 1 The Coda Centre, 189 Munster Road, London SW6 6AW
Tel: 020 7385 6333 * E-mail: contact@littletiger.co.uk * www.littletiger.co.uk